The Telephone Book

by Maida Silverman

illustrated by Ethel Gold

A GOLDEN BOOK • NEW YORK

Western Publishing Company, Inc., Racine, Wisconsin 53404

Ring, ring!
Ring, ring!
Janey's mom answers the telephone. It is
Dad calling to say that he can go with them to
buy a new phone for the family room.

After lunch, Janey calls Dad at his office.
"We will meet you in one hour," she says.

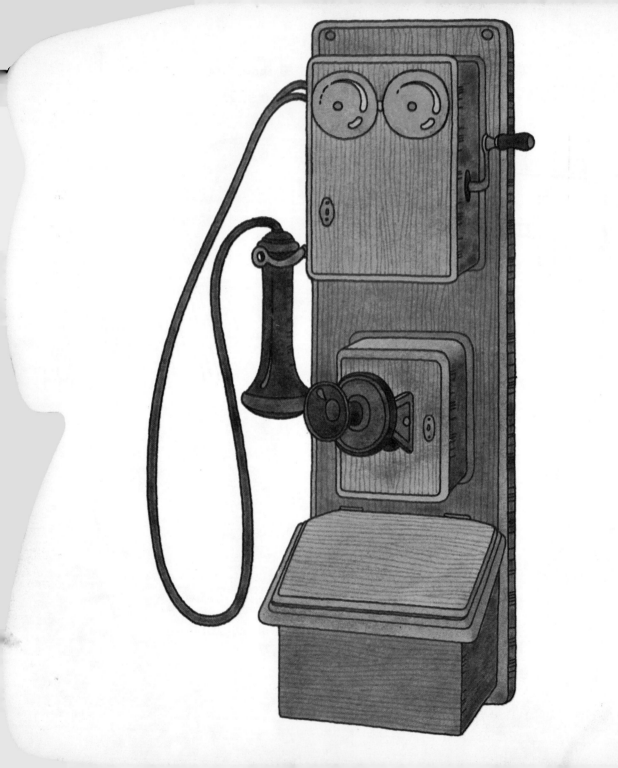

On the way to Dad's office, Janey and Mom
see an old-fashioned telephone in a store
window.

When they arrive at the office, the receptionist
calls Janey's dad on the switchboard telephone.

Mom, Dad, and Janey go to the telephone store. There are many different telephones to choose from.

There is a telephone that has jumbo push
buttons. Janey pushes one of the big buttons.

There is even a telephone that has no cord.
"I could carry this phone from room to room,"
says Mom.

Janey likes the bright red telephone best. So do Mom and Dad. This is the one they decide to buy.

On the way home, Dad calls the office to see
if there are any messages for him.

"Let's buy a toy telephone for Eric," says
Janey. So they stop at the toy store, and Janey
picks out a telephone for her little brother.

At home, Janey and Mom help Dad install
the new telephone.

"Hi, Grandma! Guess what we bought!"